Terry Treetop Finds New Friends

Tali Carmi

Terry Treetop

Finds New Friends

Written by Tali Carmi

Terry Treetop Finds New Friends

Third Edition - 09/2014

ISBN: 978-965-92331-0-6

Contact information: tbcarmi@gmail.com
Author website: www.thekidsbooks.com
Twitter: @tbcarmi

Terry was a boy with red hair and freckles,

but, no one called him just Terry.

Everybody called him Terry Treetop

because he loved climbing trees.

One day, his dad built him a tree house at the very top of his favorite tree in their backyard.

Terry was so happy that he climbed that tree to go to his new house.

He looked down on the green fields and felt like he was on top of everything.

But Terry was sad and felt lonely because he didn't have friends to play with in his new house.

He didn't want to be alone, so he decided to go on a journey to find new friends to invite to his tree house.

Terry Treetop packed all the things that he may need on this journey.

He packed a water bottle and a peanut butter and jelly sandwich that his mom made.

"Ready!" Terry said eagerly as he put on his hat. Then, he went on his way.

Terry heard the buzzing of Betty the bee.

"Hey, Betty, you sure look busy, but I have a new house on a tree. Would you like to visit there and play with me?"

"I wish I could, but I can't, Terry Treetop. I have to fill these jars with honey so I can make sweet honey buns!

Go ask the sheep named Shelly."
Terry waved goodbye to Betty and then continued on his way.

Terry got a bit thirsty from all the walking. He drank some water and then walked some more to find Shelly the sheep. A few steps later, he heard clicking sounds. It was Shelly. She was knitting.

"Hey, Shelly, you sure look busy, but I have a new house on a tree. Would you like to visit there and play with me?"

"I wish I could, but I can't, Terry Treetop. I have to knit these sweaters so children can be warm and toasty.
Go ask the chicken named Cherry."

Terry waved goodbye to Shelly and then continued on his way.

He walked for a while until he felt his tummy grumble. "Good thing I have my mom's peanut butter and jelly sandwich." Terry gobbled it all up. He burped, rubbed his belly and then he continued walking. He suddenly heard a clucking sound. It was Cherry the chicken.

"Hey, Cherry, you sure look busy, but I have a new house on a tree.
Would you like to visit there and play with me?"

"I wish I could, but I can't, Terry Treetop.
I have to fill these cartons with eggs so kids can eat omelets that are fluffy.
Go ask the cow named Kelly."

Terry waved goodbye to Cherry and then continued on his way.

Terry was getting tired from walking, but he still looked for Kelly the cow. He then asked her the same question he had been asking everyone the whole day.

"Hey, Kelly, you sure look busy, but I have a new house on a tree.
Would you like to visit there and play with me?"

"I wish I could, but I can't, Terry Treetop. I have milk cartons to fill so kids can drink milk and be healthy!
I'm sorry."

Terry waved goodbye to Kelly and then continued on his way.

Terry was feeling tired and sad.

Nobody wanted to play with him.

Everyone was so busy!

 It was almost sunset and Terry Treetop

just decided to go back home.

As he was walking back he suddenly heard,

"Meow! Meow! Help me!"

It was Kitty the kitten crying for help!

"I'm stuck on top of a tree! Someone please

help me!"

Tears fell from her big blue eyes.

Everyone heard the cry for help.

Betty the bee rushed with her jars of honey, Shelly the sheep came with a pile of sweaters, Cherry the chicken came running with her cartons of eggs and so did Kelly the cow with her cartons of milk.

They all gathered under the tree but they were afraid to climb up!

Terry came as fast as he could.

"Don't cry, Kitty. They don't call me Terry Treetop for nothing!"

He rolled up his sleeves and then climbed the tree.

"Hold on tight, I will get you down. I promise."

Kitty hugged Terry tightly.

He knew that Kitty was really scared so he climbed down from the tree slowly, step by step until he brought Kitty to safety.

When they were both on the ground, Kitty

was so happy that she gave Terry a big lick

on his face and told him:

"Thank you, Terry Treetop. You're so brave.

I will be your friend forever!"

Everyone was really impressed.

"Your name is perfect for you

Terry Treetop!

You climbed that tree quickly and you

weren't even scared. You did a really good

deed today."

Then, Betty the bee, Shelly the sheep, Cherry the chicken, Kelly the cow and Kitty the kitten followed Terry to his new tree house where they made a party for saving Kitty.

That made Terry even happier because he had finally found new friends he could play with.

Terry was not alone anymore.

THANK YOU!

This book has been created with love and joy,

and it is very important for me to know

what you think about it.

Please leave a review on Amazon.

Your thoughts mean a lot to me.

Lot's of Love
- Tali

To my dear readers:

Thank you for purchasing *Terry Treetop Finds New Friends*, the first book of my Adventure & Education Children's Books series.

I really enjoyed writing about this little boy and his encounters with farm animals, and I've already had some great feedback from kids and parents who enjoyed the story and illustrations. I hope you too enjoyed it.

I appreciate that you chose to buy and read my book over some of the others out there. Thank you for putting your confidence in me to help educate and entertain your kids.

If you and your children enjoyed *Terry Treetop Finds New Friends* and you have a couple of spare minutes now, it would really help me out if you would like to leave me a review (even if it's short) on Amazon. All these reviews really help me spread the word about my books and encourage me to write more and add more to the series!

Sincerely yours,

Tali Carmi

Other books by Tali carmi

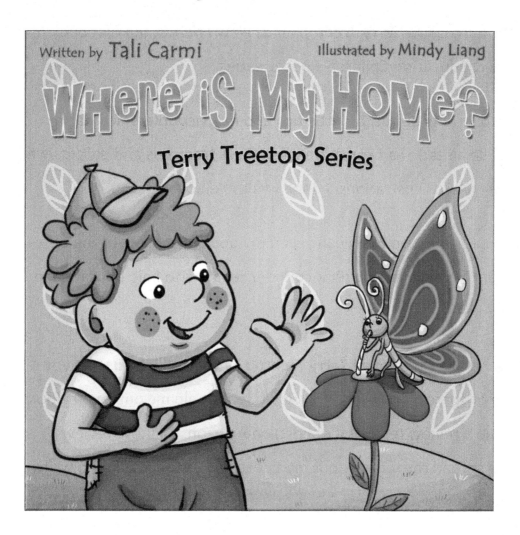

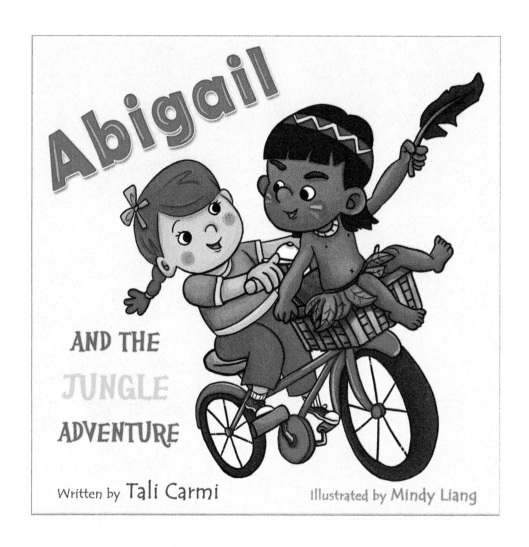

Abigail

AND THE JUNGLE ADVENTURE

Written by **Tali Carmi**   Illustrated by **Mindy Liang**

CPSIA information can be obtained
at www.ICGtesting.com
Printed in the USA
BVOW07*1204201116
468369BV00001B/1/P